# Chapter One

There once was a cat who thought
he could sing.
"My voice is so *purr*-fect," he said.
"That I will become a superstar!"

The cat's owners called him Scruff.
He wanted to be called Rex, or Tiger.
"I can't be a superstar with a name like
Scruff," he said.

He waited until everything was silent.
Completely silent.
Then he sang.

A light went on inside the house.
"They've heard me!" cried Scruff.
"My life is about to change."

At meal times, it was just as bad.
"If I'm going to be a superstar, I should
eat chicken and fresh fish," said Scruff.

But his owners gave him food from a tin
and put it in a bowl on the floor.

"I should not have to sleep in a cat basket," said Scruff. "I should have soft cushions on the very best chair."

But his owners made him sleep in a basket in the corner of the room.

A window opened and a head poked out.
"Stop that horrible noise!" it yelled.
"Do you like my singing?" said Scruff.

The head went away. A moment later,
it came back and something flew
through the air.
"Is it a soft cushion?" said Scruff.
He ran over to look.

"An empty cat food tin," he purred.
"My dirty bowl. They've thrown them
out! At last, they're going to treat
me like a superstar!"

Scruff waited for the door to open, and for his owners to welcome him back in.

The door stayed shut.

"They've had enough of you, mate,"
came a voice.
It was the dog from next door.

"Had enough of me?" cried Scruff.
"No, they haven't. They love me!"
"Well, they don't love your singing.
And neither do I. So put a sock in it,
will you?"

Scruff was so shocked, he did not know what to say. He was sure the dog was wrong. He stayed by the door for a long, long time, but nobody came.
Finally, he gave up.
"It's their loss," he sniffed. "I will go and find someone else to sing to.

# Chapter Three

Scruff set off down the road with his
tail in the air. In the next street, he heard
music coming from one of the houses.
"Those people will like my singing,"
he said. He cleared his throat
and began.

The music stopped. A window opened and something flew through the air. Scruff crept towards it. "Is it fresh fish?" It wasn't. It was an old wellington boot.

"What use is that?" he cried. "Do they think I want to be Puss-in-Boots?"

Scruff set off again, going further and
further away from home.
A ginger tom growled as he trotted by.
"Go back to where you belong," he said.
"This is *my* street."

"Can I sing to you?" asked Scruff.
He began before the cat had time to
answer, but then stopped when he saw
the cat's face.
"Get out before I chase you out,"
growled the cat, his fur standing on end.

Scruff was terrified, and ran for his life.
He did not stop until he came to a dark,
empty alley.
Then he heard a rustling noise.
It was coming from behind a black,
plastic bag.

"Who's there?" he asked.

He moved forward, ready to pounce, and
came face to face with a very large fox.
"I thought you were a mouse," said Scruff
nervously.
"Do I look like a mouse?" snarled the fox.
"No, you look like a cross fox," said
Scruff.

"Can I sing to make you happy?"
The fox snarled and, with a great leap,
he caught Scruff's tail between his teeth.

MMMEEOOOWW!

Scruff yowled in pain and ran for his life. He did not stop until he came to the edge of a river and hid among some reeds. "Why won't anyone let me sing to them?" he sniffed. "They don't know what they're missing."

# Chapter Four

It was a long time before Scruff dared to
come out. When he did, it began to rain.
"A singer should not get wet," he said.
"The rain will make my voice squeak.
I must find somewhere warm to shelter"

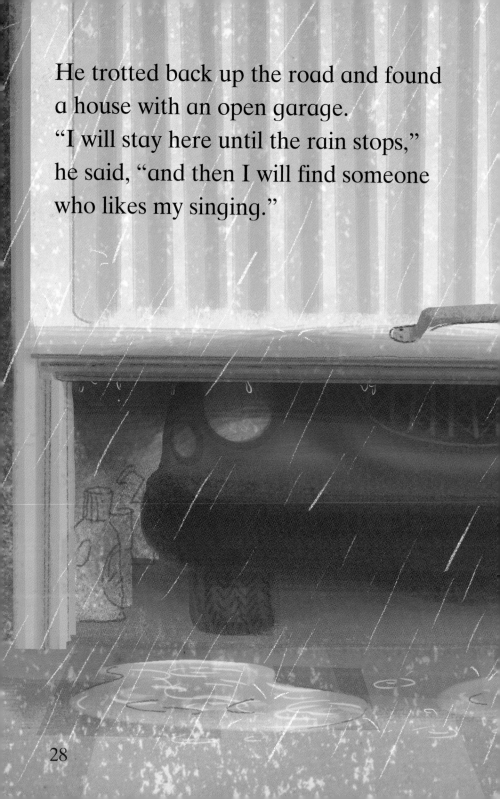

He trotted back up the road and found
a house with an open garage.
"I will stay here until the rain stops,"
he said, "and then I will find someone
who likes my singing."

The rain didn't stop.
Scruff stood by the garage door, and
watched the puddles getting bigger
and bigger.

29

Finally, he was so tired that he crept into a corner and went to sleep in a box.

After a while, he was woken by a noise.

Scruff pricked up his ears.
"That sounds like someone singing,"
he said to himself.
He trotted towards the sound.

Around the corner was a big, open park with a wall on one side. On top of the wall was a row of cats. A ginger cat was singing. In a circle, on the ground, lots of other cats were watching.

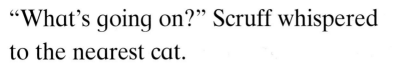

"What's going on?" Scruff whispered
to the nearest cat.
"It's the Meow Factor!" said the cat.
"We're here to choose the best singer."
Scruff could not believe it.
"Can I take part?" he asked.
"Of course," said the cat.
"Go and sit on the wall."

Scruff jumped up straight away. He was very excited, and could not wait for his turn to come. He would show them what *real* singing sounded like.

# Chapter Five

One after another, the cats sang.
Sometimes the cats on the ground
cheered, and sometimes they booed.

A grey cat tried to dance and nearly
fell off the wall.

A black and white cat forgot his words.

A tabby cat was so bad, all the other cats put their paws over their ears.

At last, it was Scruff's turn.
The cat beside him leaned over.
"Good luck," she whispered.

In the dawn
light, Scruff saw she was
the prettiest, fluffiest cat in the world.

Under his fur, Scruff blushed bright pink.
Suddenly, his legs began to tremble.
He opened his mouth to sing, but no
sound came out. All he could think about
was the pretty cat.

"Hurry up," said a big, black tom.
"We haven't got all night."

Scruff tried again, but it was no use.
His voice had disappeared. "S-sorry,"
he said. "I've got to go home."
He jumped down from the wall.

"Wait!" called a voice, but Scruff
ran away.
"Please wait," the voice called again.
Scruff stopped, and turned round.

42

It was the pretty cat.
"Why didn't you sing?" she asked.
Scruff blushed again. "I was too shy,"
he mumbled.
"Will you sing to me?" she asked.

Scruff looked into her big, green eyes.
"All right," he said.
Then he took a deep breath and sang.

"Your voice is *purr*-fect," purred the pretty cat.

"Is it?" said Scruff, shyly.

"Yes, it is," she smiled. "My name is Fluff. What's yours?"

"Rex," said Scruff, but somehow it did not sound right. "No, wait – it's Scruff. My name is Scruff."

"That's a good name," said Fluff. "Can I see you tomorrow, Scruff?"

Scruff nodded. "I'd like that," he said.

As the sun rose, both cats ran home.
Scruff could not wait to have breakfast...

and a sleep in his basket.

And that evening, his owners would
not have to push him out through the cat
flap. He would leap out all by himself.

After all, he was going to meet the prettiest, fluffiest cat in the world, and someone who liked his singing. Life could not be more *purr*-fect!